KU-769-666

This igloo book belongs to:

....

Contents

igloobooks

Published in 2019
by Igloo Books Ltd, Cottage Farm, Sywell, NN6 0BJ
www.igloobooks.com

Copyright © 2017 Igloo Books Ltd

All rights reserved. No part of this publication may be reproduced or transmitted
in any form or by any means, electronic, or mechanical, including photocopying,
recording, or by any information storage and retrieval system,
without permission in writing from the publisher.

Written by Melanie Joyce
Illustrated by Angelika Scudamore

Designed by Kerri-Ann Hulme
Edited by Caroline Richards

REX001 1218
2 4 6 8 10 9 7 5 3 1
ISBN 978-1-78905-973-1

Printed and manufactured in China

Stories for

2

Year Olds

igloobooks

Seaside Fun

Jake was at the seaside
with Mum and his sister, too.

Pip said,

It's your first time,
how exciting for you!

But there were lots of **noises** that Jake hadn't heard before.

Screech!

went the seagulls.

CRASH!

went the waves on the shore.

There was sand on Jake's beach towel and in between his toes.
The little grains got **everywhere**, even up his nose!

Jake felt a little braver when he had Pip's hand to hold.
He dipped his toe in the water and cried out,

Then underneath the water,
something green **wiggled** about.

It tickled Jake's legs.
He **squealed** and wanted to get out.

Pip said,

It's only seaweed, don't worry, hold on to me.

And before Jake knew it, he was floating in the sea!

Pip kicked her legs and **splashed.**

I'll show you what to do.

Jake copied her and giggled.

Now I'm swimming, too!

Later, Pip and Jake built a sandcastle on the sand.

Strawberry or vanilla?

asked Mum, with ice
creams in her hand.

Jake had so much **fun** playing all afternoon with Pip.
He had definitely enjoyed his very first seaside trip!

Picnic Time

In Max's neighbourhood there
was going to be a picnic lunch.
The little ones couldn't **wait** for
something nice to **munch**.

The picnic wasn't ready,
so Max **swung** from the tree.

He said,

I'll go and see if Tod
wants to play with me.

But Tod wasn't happy at all.

I'm so hungry,

he moaned.

Then his empty tummy...

...gurgled, squelched and groaned.

Zita's tummy was **grumbling.** She wanted something to chew.

Pete was in such a **flap** because he was hungry, too.

Nobody wanted to play.
They weren't in a very good mood.

Max said,

It will be alright, you just need some food!

Colin said,

You're right! Please can you make it snappy. Cupcakes, sandwiches and fruit, would make me very happy.

Everyone **ran** at once.
It was just like a **stampede**.

They shouted out happily,

At last, we're going to have a feed!

So it was that everyone...

... munched, crunched and sluuuurped.

They **bit** and **chomped** and **chewed**...

... nibbled, gulped and burped.

When the picnic was over and everyone was fed,
they played **happily** all afternoon, until it was time for bed.

Let's Play Pretend

On a beautiful bright and sunny day,
it's just the right weather to go out and play.

Let's open the dressing-up box...

... one, two, three...

... and see what's **inside** for you and me.

I can be a **sparkly** princess...

... and you can be a **king.**

We'll sit on our thrones and we won't do a thing.

Or we can be like **fierce** lions shouting out...

... ROAR!

Or wiggly snakes, **slithering** along the floor.

We can **hop, hop, hop** and preten we are frogg

crouching down low and **leaping** over logs.

I'll build us a **den** out of blankets and sticks.

You can be a **magician**
and do magic tricks.

We'll be brave explorers,
who are **never** afraid...

... but run back **giggling**
to the den that we've made.

Maybe we'll be pirates sailing out to sea?
We'd find lots of **treasure** and come home for tea.

Perhaps we'll have a picnic
and eat **lots** of treats.

Like **wobbly** jelly...

... sandwiches...

... and sweets.

We can play all afternoon, until the day is at an end.
We can be anything we want, when we **play pretend!**

Toy Box Adventure

Each evening, in the playroom, the toys were put away.
But one night they weren't sleepy at the end of the day.

Bunny said,

Let's have an adventure, come on everyone! We'll sneak out into the garden and really have some fun.

There was...

... **Bunny,**

Robot...

... **Teddy...**

... and **Sparkly Fairy,** too.

Dinosaur decided to come, and brought **bouncy** Kangaroo.

The toys **slid** on
the slide...

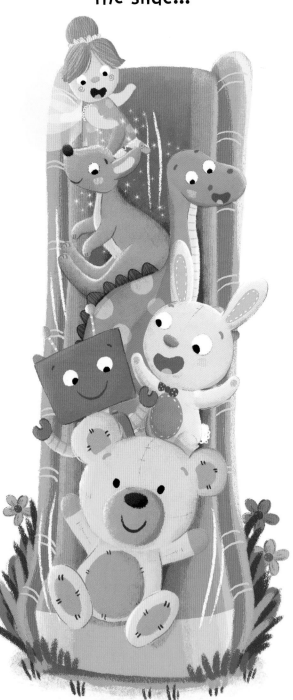

... and had such **fun**
on the swing.

They ran around the garden and **danced** in the fairy ring.

They played at chase and hide-and-seek, it was the best fun **ever**.

Dinosaur said,

I wish we could stay and play out here forever.

Sparkly Fairy told them stories, sitting on a spotty mushroom.

The toys began to feel quite sleepy and thought of their playroom.

Everyone started yawning.

Playtime is over,

Robot said.

And with that, the tired toys went happily back to bed.

Bedtime for Kit

Mummy tells Kit,

It's nearly bedtime for you.

But Kit says that she has one last thing to do.

Kit wants to go
and say goodnight,
to all her little friends
as they **cuddle** up tight.

Kit says **goodnight** to her best friend, Dee.

She blows her
a **kiss** and says,

It's from me!

Kit finds Milo settling down for the night. She says,

Goodnight Milo, sleep tight.

Kit gives a goodnight cuddle to one **last** friend. Buddy is sleepy now the day is at an end.

Kit's Mummy says,

Come on, sleepy head. You've said goodnight to everyone, now it's time for bed.

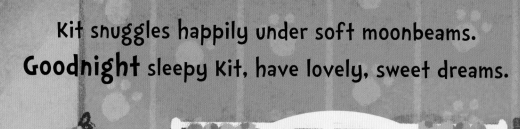
Kit snuggles happily under soft moonbeams.
Goodnight sleepy Kit, have lovely, sweet dreams.